-My Family-
My Two Dads

by Claudia Harrington
illustrated by Zoe Persico

Looking Glass Library

An Imprint of Magic Wagon
abdopublishing.com

To my Fab 4 - Emmett, Gretchen, Tess & Ken. Additional thanks to Lee Wind, for holding me to a higher standard. —CH

To my two sisters for being such fun and exciting siblings, you keep me on my toes (in a good way). —ZP

abdopublishing.com

THIS BOOK CONTAINS
RECYCLED MATERIALS

Written by Claudia Harrington
Illustrated by Zoe Persico
Edited by Heidi M.D. Elston
Designed by Candice Keimig

Library of Congress Cataloging-in-Publication Data

Harrington, Claudia, 1957- author.
  My two dads / by Claudia Harrington ; illustrated by Zoe Persico.
     pages cm. -- (My family)
  Summary: Lenny follows Jasmine for a school project and learns about her life with her two dads.
  ISBN 978-1-62402-108-4
1. Gay fathers--Juvenile fiction. 2. Fathers and daughters--Juvenile fiction. 3. Families--Juvenile fiction. [1. Gay fathers--Fiction. 2. Fathers and daughters--Fiction. 3. Family life--Fiction.]
I. Persico, Zoe, 1993- illustrator. II. Title.
  PZ7.1.H374Mt 2016
  [E]--dc23
                                    2015002655

When the bell rang at the end of the day, Miss Fish took Lenny aside. "Lenny, as class reporter, you're going home with Jasmine today. She's Student of the Week."

"Hi, Lenny. I'm Jasmine, but you can call me Jazz. Everybody does!"
"Sure, Jazz," said Lenny. **Click!** "Are we going to take the bus?"

Jazz shook her head. "Dad picks me up. Have you ever ridden in a horse trailer?"
Lenny tried not to look scared. "No."

When the trailer pulled up, Lenny grabbed his camera. **Click!**

"I'm glad we don't have to ride in the horse part!" he said.

Jazz's dad laughed. "Nice to meet you. I'm Jazz's dad. Well, the short one." He winked at Jazz. **Click!** "What's your name?"

The smells of hay and horses wafted from the back.

"Horse," said Lenny.

Jazz laughed.

Lenny's face got hot. "I mean Lenny," he said.

"You get used to the smell," said Jazz as they bumped over a long dirt road. Jazz pointed to a big barn set back from the road. "Home sweet home!"

"You live in a barn?" asked Lenny. **Click!**

Jazz smiled. "No, we live in that farmhouse right next to it."

"But it sometimes feels like we live in the barn," said Dad. "We spend a lot of time there."

"Who helps with your school projects?" asked Lenny as they hopped out of the truck.

"Papi checks my design," said Jazz as Papi swung her around in a circle. **Click!** "But he's sometimes installing his own art in a city somewhere. So Dad helps me if I need it."

"Speaking of projects," said Papi, "why don't you two pick some apples and then work on your solar systems?"

"If you grab a couple of extra apples, you can feed them to the horses," called Dad.

"Cool!" said Lenny. **Click!**

"Just keep your hand flat," said Jazz.

"Who takes care of the horses?" asked Lenny.

"Dad does, but Papi and I help sometimes," said Jazz.

"Hi, Doodles."

Click!

"Who makes your dinner?" asked Lenny as they worked on their projects.

"Papi does, if he's home. Otherwise we might have to eat oats!" laughed Jazz.

"I'm great with carrots, too," joked Dad.
"Dinner's almost ready!" yelled Papi.

"Does your dad always braid your hair?" asked Lenny. **Click!**

Jazz nodded.

"Hold still," said Dad.

"He's used to braiding the horses' tails," said Jazz. "But I like working on this end better!" joked Dad. They all laughed.

"What do you do for fun?" asked Lenny.

"Come on!" Jazz dragged him to the barn, then pressed play.

"Bow to your partner, do-si-do," called a recorded voice. **Click!**

"Who taught you to dance?" asked Lenny.
"Dad and Papi both did!" said Jazz.

"Circle left and promenade home!" called the voice.
When the last song ended, Lenny was out of breath.
"Who dusts you off?" he asked.

"Every cowboy and cowgirl for themselves!" said Papi as Dad handed out horse brushes.

"Who reads your bedtime story?" asked Lenny.

"Dad and Papi take turns," said Jazz. "And Doodles listens!"

"Who loves you best?" asked Lenny.

"We both do!" said Dad and Papi. **Click!**

Lenny ran to give his mom a hug.

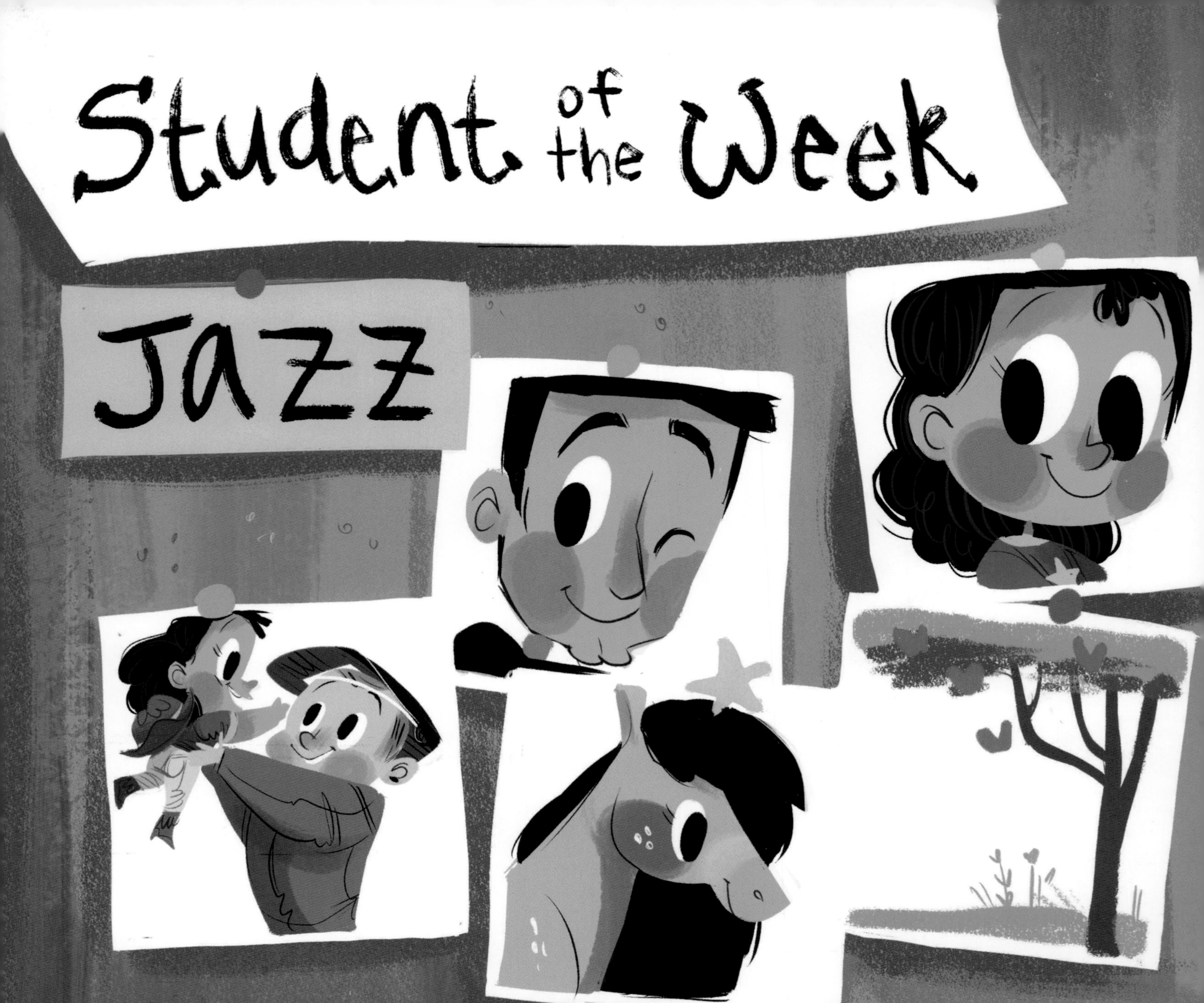
Student of the Week
JAZZ

"Good night, Student of the Week!"
said Lenny.
"Good night, twinkle toes!"
said Jazz.